WALLACE, Karen

Thunderbelle's party

For Djazia Spowers
K.W.
For Billy and Marcie,
with love
G.P-R.

First published in 2007 by Orchard Books
First paperback publication in 2008

ORCHARD BOOKS
338 Euston Road, London NW1 3BH
Orchard Books Australia
Level 17/207 Kent St, Sydney, NSW 2000

ISBN 978 1 84362 619 0 (hardback)
ISBN 978 1 84362 627 5 (paperback)

Text © Karen Wallace 2007
Illustrations © Guy Parker-Rees 2007

The rights of Karen Wallace and Guy Parker-Rees to be identified
as the author and illustrator of this work have been asserted by them
in accordance with the Copyright, Designs and Patents Act, 1988.

1 3 5 7 9 10 8 6 4 2 (hardback)
1 3 5 7 9 10 8 6 4 2 (paperback)

Printed in China

Orchard Books is a division of Hachette Children's Books,
an Hachette Livre UK company.

www.orchardbooks.co.uk

Monster Mountain

Thunderbelle's Party

Karen Wallace

Illustrated by

Guy Parker-Rees

ORCHARD BOOKS

Thunderbelle lived on Monster
Mountain. She loved dressing up,
climbing trees, cooking and eating.

But, best of all, she liked playing
with her friends.

Four other monsters lived
on Monster Mountain.
Roxorus wanted to
be a pop star.

Clodbuster liked building
things. And knocking
them down!

Mudmighty loved gardening and getting muddy.

And Pipsquawk loved hanging upside down and thinking amazing thoughts.

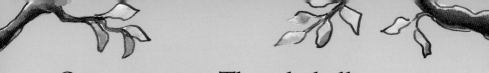

One morning Thunderbelle
woke up with a brilliant idea!
She ran outside and rang the
Brilliant Ideas gong. **Bong!**
Bong! Bong!

The other monsters came as fast as they could. Roxorus zoomed up on his skateboard.

Clodbuster swung in on a rope.

Mudmighty slid down on some watermelon.

"Where is Pipsquawk?"
cried Thunderbelle.
"Here I am!" squawked Pipsquawk.
"What is your brilliant idea?"

"A party!" cried Thunderbelle.
"Today! In my garden!"
All the monsters roared
and stomped.

What a brilliant idea!

Then Pipsquawk had another idea.
"How about a fancy dress party?"
The monsters roared and stomped
even louder.

"Pipsquawk! You are so clever!"
cried Thunderbelle. And she ran
off to get things ready.

Thunderbelle made loads of little sandwiches.

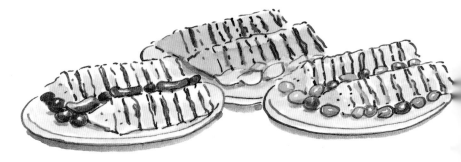

It was fun to bake lots and lots of fairy cakes and ice them with different-coloured icing.

But there was one hard thing to do.
And that was choosing what
to wear.

Thunderbelle's house was full of
cupboards. And every cupboard
was full of lovely dresses.

15

There were shiny
ones and silky ones.

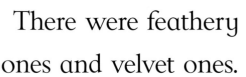

There were feathery
ones and velvet ones.

And there were
shoes and
hats and
necklaces.

16

But nothing was right for a fancy
dress party. Poor Thunderbelle!
She looked in every cupboard.

Then to cheer herself up she drank three glasses of lemonade and ate a plate of fairy cakes.

"Pink icing always helps me make up my mind," said Thunderbelle.

But the pink icing did not help.
Thunderbelle still could not decide
what to wear. So she drank five
mugs of tea and ate another plate
of fairy cakes.

"White icing always helps me think," said Thunderbelle. But the white icing didn't help.
So Thunderbelle drank seven mugs of hot chocolate and ate another plate of fairy cakes.

"Green icing and cherries always give me ideas," said Thunderbelle. And sure enough the last plate of fairy cakes did the trick.

Suddenly Thunderbelle remembered the dressing-up box under the stairs.

A fairy costume was inside!
Thunderbelle put it on. She
looked fantastic! (It was only
a little bit tight!)

Soon all the other monsters arrived.
Everyone wanted to help.

Clodbuster made
a special dance floor.

Mudmighty brought a basket of
fruit and vegetables.

Roxorus set up his
Monster Music
Machine.

And Pipsquawk thought
up some new tunes
to play.

There was only one thing
missing. "Where is Thunderbelle?"
roared Roxorus.
"Here I am!" cried Thunderbelle. But
when she tried to go into the garden
she could not get through the door!
She was too full of fairy cakes!

Poor Thunderbelle!
She pushed
and pulled.

She shoved and
squeezed. But it
was no good.

She was stuck!
"What shall
I do?" she cried.

Then Pipsquawk had an amazing thought. "We'll knock down the door!" All the monsters cheered! "Pipsquawk! You are so clever!" they cried.

Soon there was a hole where
Thunderbelle's door had been!

Thunderbelle ran onto the dance floor. "Welcome to my party!" she cried and spun round and round. The monsters jumped and danced around her.

Pipsquawk turned up the music full blast! It was a brand new tune especially for Thunderbelle! It was called the FUNKY FAIRY CAKE ROCK!

Monster Mountain

All priced at £4.99. Monster Mountain books are available from
all good bookshops, or can be ordered direct from the publisher:
Orchard Books, PO BOX 29, Douglas IM99 1BQ. Credit card orders
please telephone 01624 836000 or fax 01624 837033 or visit our website:
www.orchardbooks.co.uk or e-mail: bookshop@enterprise.net for details.

To order please quote title, author and ISBN and your full name and address.
Cheques and postal orders should be made payable to 'Bookpost plc.'
Postage and packing is FREE within the UK
(overseas customers should add £2.00 per book).

Prices and availability are subject to change.